The Savernake Big Belly Oak

Written by

Barbara Townsend

Illustrated by Chantal Bourgonje

Second edition published by Savernake Press 2016.
First edition published by Savernake Press 2012.

Savernake Press
Burbage Wiltshire SN8 3AN
Website:- www.savernakepress.weebly.com
E-mail:- babstownsend@hotmail.com
Illustrated in Wiltshire by Chantal Marie Bourgonje. www.cfordesign.co.uk
Printed by Bulpitt Print Andover, on paper, which is fully recyclable, biodegradable and contains fibre from forests meeting the Forest Stewardship Council principles and criteria (FSC).

Acknowledgements

Many thanks to the following, without whose help this book would remain unpublished.

My Granddaughter Issy, who unwittingly inspired me to get this book started. My family, in spite of my doubts, supported and provided encouragement.

My illustrator – Chantal Marie Bourgonje. It must have been fated that we lived in the same village. Thank you so much for your support. Your drawings are simply perfection.

To friends and family who read and gave constructive criticism – Thank you.

To my husband Ian, who believed in me, I love you.

Finally to the Big Belly Oak. "Hang in there old man."

There is a tree so wide and old
It has seen many things, things untold
A thousand years and it still grows
How long will it remain, no one knows
Look after the trees they are our future
Those magnificent giants of Mother Nature

By Barbara Townsend 2012

CONTENTS

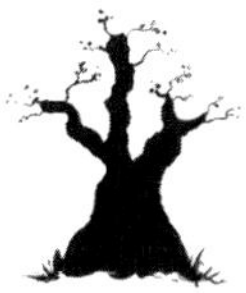

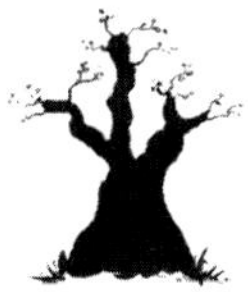

Story time for the piglets

Mighty trees grow in the Savernake Forest; however, one particular tree is extraordinarily different.

It has grown tall and strong for many years, now it bulges under its great weight. Its wide, big-bellied trunk has a gaping hole like a deep, dark mouth. Gnarled branches twist outwards like wild hair. Some people would say it's a scary, ugly tree.

Despite its looks, the tree is special. It has magical powers. Forest animals shelter inside its cavernous big belly trunk, feeling safe and secure. Everything a scared little creature could wish for is right there, inside the tree.

The aged oak is known as Tree to his forest friends. Although many trees grow around him, Tree didn't realize that they too have the same powers as him.

On one particular day a strange sound filled the air, a noise that became louder and closer to Tree. He had heard loud noises before, such as thunder and lightning, crashing and flashing brightly across the sky, the downpour of rain splashing loudly through his leaves and the strong winds, blowing and howling, bending his branches making them creak and groan.

This wasn't the normal natural noises of the forest; these were sounds of tearing, ripping, dragging, and there were many loud voices.

The sounds grew louder and closer, and Tree watched as bulldozers, trucks, tractors and men headed his way. The menacing looking bulldozers were tearing down trees and large tractors were dragging them away.

Enormous trucks were tipping stones noisily onto the ground creating a road. Closer and closer. Tree watched in disbelief as they headed his way.

The wild boar piglet twins, Rory and Horton, ran to Tree. "What's that horrible noise?" they both squealed. "We are so frightened."

"Hide inside me," whispered Tree. The piglets quickly ran inside. Tree used his magical powers; any creature that sheltered inside his large trunk would be right at home. Plenty of food to eat, dry straw to sleep on and for the two small frightened piglets, a muddy wallow to splash and play in. Both piglets ran to a cosy bed of straw, snuggled up and waited nervously.

Whenever Tree's friends were sheltering inside his big belly trunk, he would tell them stories, making them feel safe or just to cheer them up.

His stories were of long ago in the forest. He told them of Knights and Kings, dressed in their finest armour, with lances held high, flags streaming behind them, racing through the forest on their mighty horses.

That day, Tree told the story of King Henry the Eighth who married Jane Seymour. Safely snuggled up, the piglets were feeling secure so Tree began.

The King, riding out on his stallion, looked magnificent in his flowing finery. The King enjoyed hunting in the Savernake Forest and had visited many times.

That day, he noticed a beautiful girl, whose father owned the forest. He stopped and spoke to her. "What is your name?" He said gently, trying not to scare her.

"Jane," she replied shyly with a curtsey, "Jane Seymour." The King fell in love with the beautiful girl and they were married. Jane became Queen of England.

Tree told this story many times and his friends never tired of it. He whispered the story to the two small piglets, distracting them from the strange noises outside.

The bulldozers were so close and loud, Tree thought they would tear him down too. So he closed his eyes. As Tree waited the noise faded. He slowly and gradually opened his eyes. To his relief the trucks, diggers, bulldozers and men were gone. What remained, shining and twisting away into the distance like a long black slithery smooth snake was a new road.

"It's safe to come out now," Tree said to the twins with a sigh. Slowly, the piglets crept outside and looked at the dark winding road. The steam from the hot tar billowed upwards, filling the air with a strange pungent smell.

"Roads are dangerous," Tree explained to the twins. He told them about the cars, trucks and buses that would soon drive along the new road, all in a great hurry. "You must take great care so you don't get hurt," said Tree. Rory and Horton listened and said they understood. Running off into the forest, the twins were glad to be away from the strange smell.

The accident that didn't happen

Tree stood sentinel beside the road. He appeared to be guarding the forest against the traffic, which raced and rumbled past him each day.

He knew by the sound of wheels on the road, which vehicle would be passing soon, especially the milk trucks collecting milk from the farms or the school buses carrying the children to and from school each day. Today he heard the school bus. "Something is wrong," he said aloud, "dreadfully wrong."

One of the large tyres was beginning to deflate and Tree knew it. "The children could be in danger," said Tree. "I MUST STOP THE BUS." Tree had a plan. The wintertime had left Tree with old loose branches and twigs that the winds had failed to clear for him.

Tree began to shiver and shake himself violently. He heaved his old branches backwards and forwards as hard as he could and gradually, the old loose twigs and branches began to fall to the ground creating an untidy mound blocking the road. Soon the school bus appeared and came to a sudden halt. The driver came to inspect the blocked road.

"What a mess," he said aloud. "These children will be late for school today," he muttered crossly. As the driver headed back to the bus, he spotted the deflating tyre and realised there could have been a terrible accident.

A breakdown truck soon arrived and the children watched the new tyre being changed from a safe distance. With the road cleared and the school children back on the bus, they drove safely away.

All the children cheered, excited to tell of their morning's adventure.

Tree saves the baby crow

Tree loved the crisp cold spring mornings; everywhere looked fresh and new. Many green leaves were already beginning to bud on Tree's branches and he knew that soon the birds would be looking for a good place to build their new nests.

He hoped they would choose his branches again. Talon and Wing already knew where they would build theirs.

The crows came to see Tree and asked if they could choose a branch. "Oh yes please," said Tree, who always looked forward to the hustle and bustle of the noisy crows in his branches.

Talon and Wing were soon picking up small twigs, placing and weaving them between Tree's branches. They gathered soft moss and packed it tightly between the twigs. Soon the nest would be ready, cosy and warm waiting for new eggs.

On a bright chilly morning, one by one the baby crows pushed their way out of the eggs and began to squawk hungrily. Talon and Wing had three babies this year and they were hungry.

The two crows flew backwards and forwards with beaks full of fat, tasty worms for their hungry chicks. "Phew this is hard work," said Wing. They both looked forward to the evenings so they could rest and snuggle up in the cosy nest together.

That night it rained. Talon stretched his wings over the chicks to keep them dry. The rain became heavy and the wind began to blow harder and harder. Tree's branches began to sway so much that the crows were sure the nest would fall. "HELP," squawked Talon, "the nest is going to fall."

"Don't worry," said Tree. Tree slowly and gently wrapped his branches around the nest protecting the precious family from falling. "Thank you," said the crows.

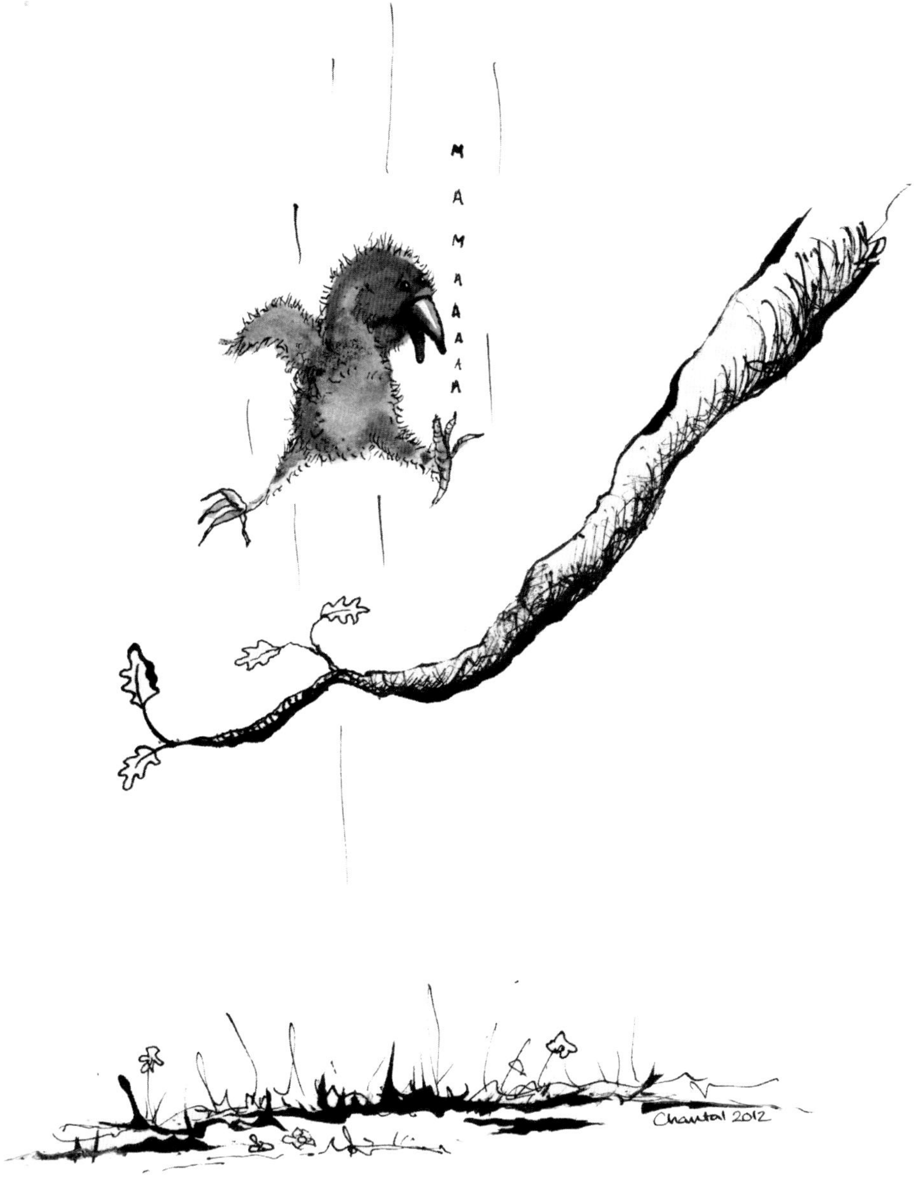
MAMAAAAAM
Chantal 2012

However, the wind grew stronger and stronger and although the nest remained safe, one of the baby crows fell out. Down, down, down it fell. "NO," Talon screamed. Talon couldn't leave the nest for fear of the other young crows falling.

Tree heard the scream, quickly stretched out one of his branches, reaching out to save the tiny crow. Tree's twigs twisted, turned, and gently caught the baby, lifting the frightened chick back into his nest.

"Here you go little man." said Tree, "Hold on tight next time." Although the wind blew hard, the crows were safe, snuggled together, waiting for the storm to blow over.

Bracken and Fern

In the gentle spring breeze, bluebells waved their tiny bells, creating a moving carpet of blue on the forest floor. At this time of year, mothers would bring their new babies to show them the special hiding place deep inside Tree's big belly trunk.

One spring morning a mother deer brought her two new fawns to meet Tree.

This is Bracken and this is Fern," she said proudly, nudging them gently towards Tree. "Come inside," said Tree. "Don't be frightened." Bracken and Fern nervously trotted in and were delighted to find everything two young deer could ever wish for.

There were ferns to sleep on, tasty leaves and grass to nibble and plenty of room to practise running and jumping on their long wobbly legs. "Oh this looks fun," they both bleated as they explored inside Tree. Running around, they found little areas to snuggle and hide in; they nibbled on leaves and juicy grass and felt right at home.

To help make the fawns feel welcome, Tree decided to tell them the story of the famous white stag that once ruled the Forest. When the fawns were snuggled up in a patch of ferns, Tree began.

Long ago a brave white stag came to the Savernake Forest. This mighty looking stag fought many battles to earn his rightful place to rule.

He ruled with courage, strength and kindness and the creatures of the forest respected him and obeyed his commands without question. Peace and calm filled the forest.

"Since that day long ago," said Tree, "there has always been a white stag ruling in our forest and one day one of you will take his place."

Bracken and Fern looked puzzled.

"We both have brown fur with spots," they both said looking at each other.

Tree chuckled to himself; he had already used his magical powers to decide which of the fawns would grow to be the next mighty white stag of the forest.

"Trust me." said Tree, "Now run along and find your mother."
Tree smiled. In the spring sunshine, he could already see flecks of white hair beginning to grow on one of the youngsters.

Bracken trotted away unaware of his future.

The badgers and the giant goblin

Tree loved the way the sunbeams danced through his branches. His leaves rustled and quivered in the gentle summer breeze and he could feel the warmth of the sun as it splashed over him.

He marvelled at the sun going down in the evenings, creating long shadows on the forest floor. They appeared like giants that stretched and stretched along the ground.

Two young badgers raced up to Tree. He kept quiet. Buttercup and her brother Clover had escaped their mother's watchful eye whilst she gathered fresh bedding for their den.

"This is the Tree," whispered Clover, "the one I told you about. If you run around it twelve times the Giant Goblin will appear."

"But why would you want that to happen?" said Buttercup nervously, keen to return to her mother, but wanting to appear brave to her adventurous brother.

"I'm not scared of the Giant Goblin," said Clover puffing out his chest. "Let's do it." "Come on," he shouted. Buttercup cowered in the long grass. Clover ran round and around the Tree. "1, 2, 3," he said loudly, "4, 5, 6," even louder, "7, 8, 9," now out of breath. "10, 11, 12."

"STOP! Let's go home," said Buttercup now shaking with fear. Clover came to a halt, and waited for the Giant Goblin to appear.

Tree, without warning, shook and waved his branches and leaves as hard as he could, making them creak, groan and rustle loudly. The frightened badgers jumped.

They both ran in fear of the Giant Goblin and rushed back to their mother as fast as their little legs could carry them, much too terrified to look back. Tree chuckled to himself. "Silly Badgers, they won't be doing that again in a hurry, that's for sure, and maybe they will stay with their Mother next time."

Sammy and the Broomstick

The trees were wearing their autumn overcoats in beautiful reds and gold. The forest appeared to be on fire with colour.

The misty cold mornings felt eerie and the dark shadows in the evenings danced around as the low setting sun shone orange and red in the sky. Tree loved the changing colours; he would shiver with delight as the mist swirled around his branches.

Gathering fallen leaves for his cosy bed, Sammy the hedgehog kept busy. He needed enough to keep him warm throughout the winter months while he slept. He had a place deep inside Tree's large big belly trunk, perfect for a spiny little creature.

There were thousands of leaves to choose from and hundreds of juicy worms to fatten up on to see him though the long cold days and nights. Once Sammy had put the finishing touches to his cosy bed and had eaten so many worms he thought he would pop, he wriggled his fat little body into the middle of his leafy bed until he felt comfy. "Time for my story," said Sammy. Tree would always tell him the same story each year to help him settle for his long winter sleep. Tree began.

Long ago in the forest, a family of hedgehogs lived in a hollow log near a stream.

One cold clear moon-lit night one young hedgehog called Sammy woke up to the sound of someone tapping on the log. Slowly, quietly, he crept outside to investigate. To his surprise, he saw a broomstick tapping the log.

"Go on, go on," said sleepy Sammy, who loved this story about himself. "Ok ok," said Tree, "snuggle down and I will continue."

The broomstick tapped again.
"What do you want?" Sammy whispered.

"It's such a good night for flying," said the broomstick, "I thought you might like to join me?"

"I would, but I don't know how to fly," replied Sammy.

"Ah, but I do," said the broomstick, "hold on tight to me and I will show you." Sammy climbed onto the broom and wrapped his little paws tightly around it.

"What's your name?" asked Sammy now feeling a little scared. "Ander." He replied. "Ready? Let's go." Ander whooshed high into the air, swerving sharply to avoid hitting the tree tops.

In the moonlight Sammy could see the forest stretching far into the distance. "The forest is really big," whispered Sammy. He could see long pathways crisscrossing and leading out of the forest.

Ander flew towards a bright light shining from the centre of the

forest. Sammy held on tightly as the broom headed downwards. As they flew closer, Sammy could see a large cauldron and around it stood three witches.

He had heard stories that witches lived in the forest but he didn't believe it. The witches began dancing around the large, black, steaming cauldron and chanted magic spells.

"Why are we heading towards the witches?" Sammy shouted, shaking with fear.
"Ha Ha Ha! " said the broomstick, "they need something for their cauldron and you're it."
"No No No!" Sammy screamed and began to struggle violently.

BANG.

Sammy had rolled and fallen out of his leafy bed and bumped his head. He'd only been dreaming after all.

Tree looked at Sammy, asleep in his cosy bed and knew that he never heard the ending of the story; he was always fast asleep at the part where Sammy flew on the broomstick.

"I'm glad he's asleep," said Tree. "Wouldn't want to scare my little friend now would I?"

"Sleep well Sammy."

Skip's first snowfall

The fresh snowfall glistened and sparkled like tiny diamonds in the early morning sun. The air crisp and cold, Tree could feel the chilly snow as it lay on his branches and drifted around the base of his large trunk. "It's so beautiful," Tree sighed.

The snow yet undisturbed lay like a soft blanket covering the ground. That soon changed. Skip, the squirrel, and his friends raced down nearby trees where they had slept in cosy hollows.

"Wow," said excited Skip, who hadn't seen snow before.

"Yippee," said the others.

Snow flew everywhere as the friends scampered up and down the trees, jumping from branch to branch making the snow fall in clouds of dust, then jumping into drifts of snow where they completely disappeared.

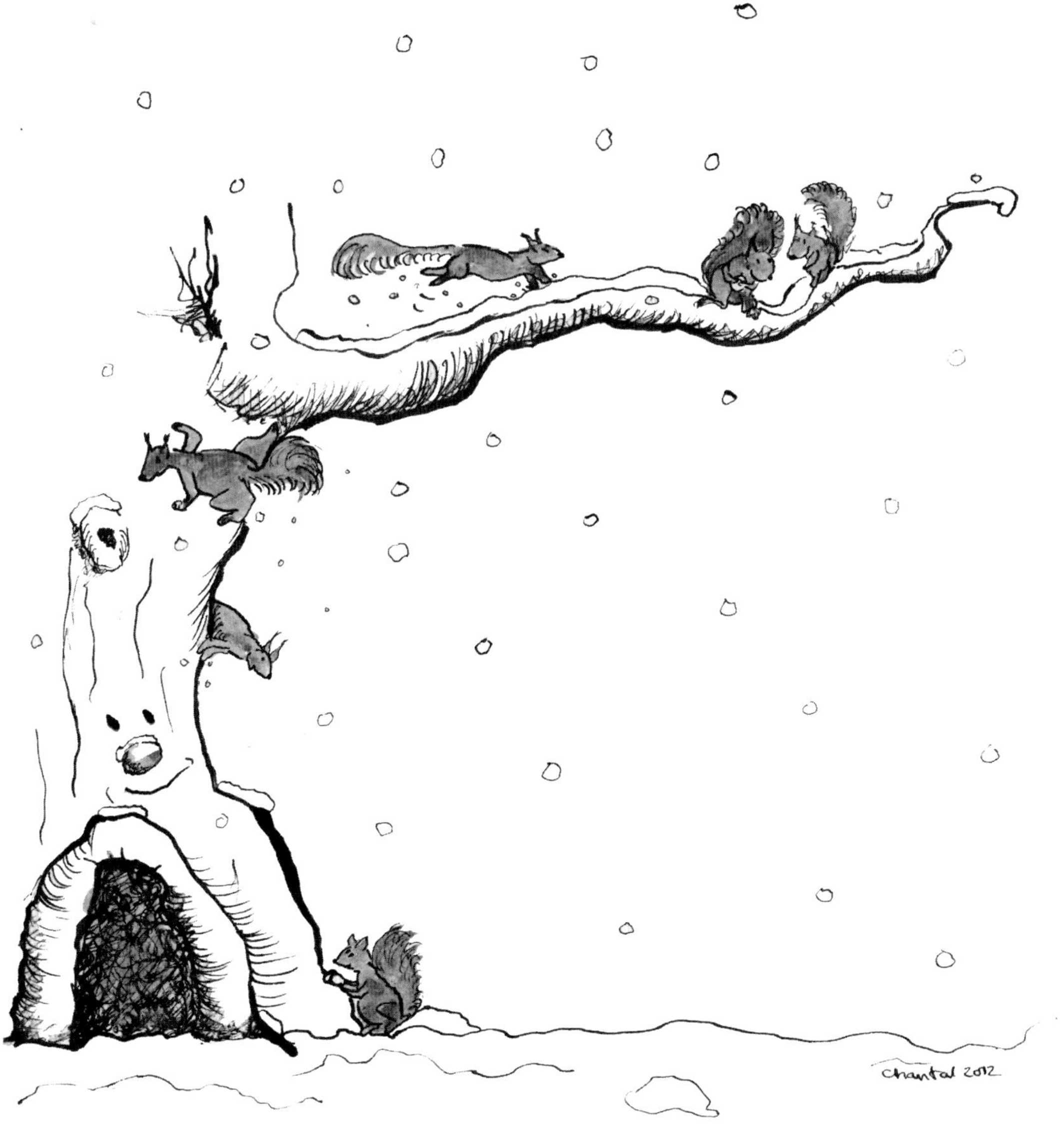
chantal 2012

The squirrels eventually stood panting and out of breath. Tree chuckled, as he looked at the soggy group. "I think you'd better come inside and dry yourselves," he said, "you do look extremely damp."

The squirrels scampered inside and stood dripping, creating a large puddle around them. Looking inside Tree's cavernous big belly trunk, their eyes became wide as they saw everything young squirrels could ever wish for.

Piles of acorns, heaped into corners and some rolling loosely around the floor. There were cosy piles of dry grass to snuggle in, plenty of old bark to gnaw on, keeping their teeth good and sharp to crack open the acorns.

"We're hungry," they all shouted together. "Can we have some of these please?" they said politely.

"Of course you can," replied Tree, knowing he had a plan for these little chaps. "I need you to do me a favour though," pausing for their response.

"Yes anything." Skip said.

"Not only you Skip, all of you."

"What do we have to do?" they said anxiously, eager to pounce on the acorns.

"Well," said Tree, "you have to come back when the snow has melted, take some of the acorns and bury them in the forest. You can then hunt for them during the winter when you're hungry. Can you do that for me?"

"Of course we can," they said eagerly, amazed at Tree's generosity. Tree chuckled to himself. He knew that squirrels forget where they stash and bury most of their acorns in the forest.

These little gardeners would be responsible for planting little oak trees, which would shoot up from the forgotten acorns in springtime. "Enjoy," said Tree, smiling knowingly as the group tucked in.

The others, Tree is not alone

For over 1000 years Tree has stood in the forest.

On one calm and quiet day and feeling alone, his thoughts wandered. His big belly trunk, gnarly branches and his leaves began to fizz and sparkle. His roots quivered and seemed to reach further and deeper into the forest.

Tree suddenly heard voices, many voices. "Who's there?" Tree said surprised.

"It's us," said the voices.

Who's us?" Tree tried to see where the voices were coming from.

"We're the others," said one voice.

"I don't understand," said Tree, "what others?"

"I am King of Limbs."
"I am Dukes Vaunt."
"I am Old Paunchy."
"I am Spider."
"I am Crockmere."

The names kept coming. "We are like you," they told him. "We have always wanted to talk to you but you didn't know how to listen to us.

We are the other big Oak Trees in the forest, just like you." Tree's leaves fizzed even more. He could sense them, could almost touch them, like a new source of energy surging through his old limbs. "We have so much to tell you," they said. Tree knew he would no longer be alone.

A4

Amity Oak

Amity Drive

Meadow

Birch Copse

King of Limbs

Crockmere Oak

Pond

Red Vein Bottom

Meadow

Duke's Vaunt

Meadow

Drive

Grand Avenue

The Gallops

Cheval Bottom

Oak Tree

Arboretum

Meadow

8 Walks

Meadow

Twelve O'Clock

Saddle Oak

Braydon Oak

Sawit Ride

New King Oak

Queen Oak

Cathedral Oak

Long Harry

White Road

Church Walk

Old Paunchy

Great Lodge Drive

food prog

Charcoal Burners
Column Ride

Pond

Twelve Oak Drive

Ailesbury Column

To Marlborough

A346

Cadley

Tree!

To Burbage

Map <u>not</u> to an exact scale
Only main roads and paths are noted

44

When you travel through the Savernake Forest, look out for Tree and give him a wave, he is the one with the exceptionally big belly. You will make an old tree incredibly happy.

Also available- written by Barbara Townsend and illustrated by Chantal Bourgonje

'The Oaks of Savernake and the Legendary Ghosts'

They are gentle giants with powers far beyond our understanding. Venerable veteran oak trees stand in the ancient forest of Savernake. Over 1000 years old, many have shrunk under their own great weight and have become wide and gnarly, their immense size bending and twisting them out of shape giving them the appearance of demons and monsters.

For children 6 to 11 years

'Harriet'

Harriet dares to be different. The unseen force that drives her and the colony disappears, leaving the bees confused and vulnerable. Their lives devastated by a deadly attack, this brave honey bee leads a group to safety and journeys to find a new home and her destiny.

For children 7 to 11 years

"Old Harry Rock and Tales of the Jurassic Coast"

Old Harry stands sentinel, as though protecting the Jurassic Coast against the onslaught of the sea.
His surrounding chalk, like a sponge, soaks up visions, myths, legends and stories, storing them as memories in the cliffs and deep within the sea bed, like long lost fossils waiting to be discovered.
Old Harry has powers and can tap into this energy to rescue humans and sea creatures in peril.

For children 7 to 11 years

www.savernakepress.weebly.com - babstownsend@hotmail.com